The Seed

By

Denise Hill

DH Publishing Company
P.O. Box 333
Indianapolis, IN 46250

Titles under DH Books
Love of a Lifetime
Double Crossed
Scandalous
Envy
Torn
The Window
The Seed
The Church Needs To Do Better
Walking On Water
She Can She Will She Wins
Right On Time

DH Books

Acknowledgment

I would like to that my God for giving me the knowledge, the wisdom, and the energy to write another book. This is my seventh book. Who would have told me that I would be living my best life doing what I love to do.

I want to thank my support system, my son Daniel Powell and my daughter Devin Hill.

I want to thank my other supporters who have supported me with your purchase.

Prologue

That night, Larry tossed and turned most of the night until sleep came upon him. He fell into a deep sleep when he felt aroused. Larry felt the lips of someone wrapped around his penis. He enjoyed the feel of plump lips moving up and down him and when she climbed on top of him, and rode him. It was like heaven. The feeling was so intense, but he was enjoying every bit, and when it was over, he became petrified at what he saw. It was a monster dressed in red with horns and a long tail. Larry was so afraid that he fell out of bed and was fighting and yelling when Brandy walked in.

Brandy stood at the door as Larry fought with his sheet and was yelling, "Get away from me! Please get away from me!"

Chapter One

"**G**ood night ladies and have a pleasant weekend. Oh Brandy, before I forget, can you make a note to call Todd Radcliffe, the first thing on Monday morning to reschedule our Tuesday meeting to Friday." Luke asked on his way out.

"Sure thing, Mr. Wright," Brandy said.

Luke stepped off the elevator and was walking to his black BMW. He pushed the button on his key fob to unlock the door. He walked over to his car, opened the back door, and placed his briefcase on the back seat. When Luke turned around, he found a tall, dark man standing in front of him.

"Damn man, you scared me."

The man stood there looking intensely at Luke.

"Can I help you with something?"

The man's eyes turned jet black, and his face changed. Luke thought he was on drugs or something.

"I don't have any cash on me. Here, take my watch," Luke said as he fumbled with his watch.

"Do I look like I want your watch?"

The man's strong African accent frightened Luke.

"I don't know what you want, but please, don't hurt me, I have a family."

The man walked closer to Luke and with his eyes; he burned a hole right through Luke's forehead. The man watched as Luke's lifeless body fell to the ground. The man reached over and grabbed Luke's keys, wallet, and took off in his car.

An hour later, Luke's secretary stepped off the elevator and was walking toward her car when she found him lying there.

Two weeks later

All was quiet on this warm summer afternoon when out of nowhere an aircraft appeared in the sky and hovered over a deserted field in the middle of nowhere and as it got lower and lower, the dust from the field blinded the operator of the aircraft. The aircraft operator landed the aircraft in the middle of the deserted field. This time landing was much smoother than normal. As the operator exited the aircraft, she saw her brother Benny parked across the street waiting for her arrival. She took slow steps toward him and as she did, her body transformed from an alien into a beautiful woman. Her brother sat in the car and watched as she walked across the street to his car and got in.

Benny, tall, dark, and handsome with an athletic build who stood at 6 feet 5 with a bold head. He looked like Michael Jordan when Michael was younger.

"You still can't handle that baby right."

"I'm getting better," Alex said.

Alex reached for her seat belt.

"Now show me one more time how this works."

Benny shook his head and laughed.

"Pull it across your chest and slide it in the latch right there."

"Oh my God! Leave it to those humans to come up with such crap," Alex said as she tried fastening her seat belt.

"It would help if you would look at what you're doing."

Alex looked over at her brother and smiled and then looked down at the seat belt latch.

"See, you're going to have to learn some patience."

Two days later

Larry rushed home from work, showered, and changed into something fresh because he knew how much Brandy hated seeing him in his dirty work clothes. He rushed home because today was their anniversary. They had been married for three years. Larry wanted everything to be perfect. He hired a friend who was a professional chef to make a special dinner for their anniversary. He had everything set up from lite jazz, food, wine, chocolates, roses, and a special gift. He went all out. He had some rose petals and candles leading from the front door and upstairs to the bathroom where he had a nice hot bath awaiting her.

Larry walked over to look out the window when he heard a car, but to his dismay, it was not Brandy. Larry was nervous about this evening because he had a new ring for Brandy and he hoped she liked it. Their relationship started out great, but over the last couple of months, things had been a little rocky. He wanted things back on track and thought this ring will do the trick. He loved Brandy with all his heart and wanted to spend the rest of his life with her.

Larry continued to pace back and forth in front of the living room window, checking his watch every five minutes. An hour had gone by and still no word from Brandy. He called her and her phone went straight to voicemail. By this time Larry was worried. He went to go look for her, but first, he dashed upstairs, blew out the candles before hopping into his car.

As Larry made his way onto the interstate his phone rang and without looking, he answered his phone.

"I was worried about you, especially when my calls went straight to voicemail."

"Sorry bro, wrong person. I was just calling you to see how things turned out, but I guess I know the answer to that. What's going on, man?"

"She never came home and my calls are going straight to voicemail. I'm on my way to her job as we speak. I got a bad feeling about this."

"Well, let me know if I can do anything," Jarrod said.

"Thanks, man. I'll hit you up later."

Larry pulled into the parking lot and immediately spotted Brandy's car. He parked right next to her, exited the car, and walked furiously into the building.

The security guard approached him before heading toward the elevators.

"Can I help you, Sir?"

"I'm here to see my wife, Brandy Jones."

"I'm sorry, but Mrs. Jones isn't here."

Larry gave the security guard a puzzled look and then looked over his shoulder and pointed to her car.

"Her car is right out front."

The security guard picked up the sign-out sheet.

"She left about two hours ago with someone."

"With whom?"

"I'm not at liberty to say."

"Man, I just want to make sure she's okay. Today is our anniversary. I have been calling and calling and her phone goes straight to voicemail. This is not like her."

The security guard hesitated, but told Larry what he knew.

"I overheard her and her companion talking about going over to Memory's Bar & Grill off of 71st and Michigan Road."

"Thanks."

Larry headed out of the building as the security guard shook his head.

Larry sat in the parking lot waiting to see who Brandy walked out with. He was busy checking his text messages that he almost missed Brandy walking out. Larry looked up just in time to see Brandy and her new boss walking to his car.

"Ain't this a bitch! I knew it. I knew something was going on between those two."
Larry hit his hand against the steering wheel. Filled with anger, Larry hopped out of the car and walked swiftly toward the two.

"I'm so glad I have seen this with my own eyes. Now you can stop telling me I'm being paranoid. How could you do this to me? Huh, Brandy?"

"Larry, what are you talking about? It's not what you think. We went out for drinks to celebrate."

"To celebrate, don't you think you should have been celebrating with your husband, seeing that it's our three-year anniversary?"

"Oh, my God! I forgot," Brandy put her hand up to her mouth.

"Larry, baby, I'm so sorry! Please forgive me." Brandy walked toward Larry and reached out for him, but he moved out of her reach.

"It's my fault, man. I talked her into coming out to celebrate with me. She helped me win this big client. I just wanted to show my appreciation, Benjamin said."

"I just bet you did," Larry walked back to his car angry and heartbroken. He left the two standing.

Denise Hill- The Seed

Chapter Two

When Larry arrived home, he grabbed a bottle of wine and headed for the den. Larry was a very handsome and nice guy. Sometimes too nice. He stood at 6 feet tall with jet black wavy hair with eyes the color of honey. He looked like he could have been mixed with a little Indian.
Larry pulled out his phone and called Jarrod.

"Man, I can't believe her. She has never forgotten before, but you know ever since she started working for that dude, things between us have changed. She makes me feel like my profession as an auto mechanic isn't good enough for her anymore. She's constantly bragging about Ben, about how much money he makes, what type of car he drives and not to mention his home."

"What the fuck! How does she even know anything about his home, anyway?"

"That's what I'm talking about. She's sleeping with this dude."
Larry threw the empty wine bottle across the room.
Brandy walked in just as the bottle went flying across the room and shattered into pieces. Brandy was an average-looking girl who should be lucky to have someone like Larry. She stood at 5 feet 6 with short hair and was a little overweight, but Larry thought the world of her.

"What is your damn problem!" Brandy yelled as she made her way into the den.

"Man, let me call you later."

"Be cool, bro. Do nothing that you will regret later."

"Alright, later."

"Aw, so you decide to grace me with your presence? Please, don't do me any fuckin favors. You should have stayed with that nigga."

"Larry, don't be like that. I told you how sorry I was for forgetting our anniversary. What more can I say or do?"Larry gave Brandy an evil eye as he walked past her and headed upstairs to the bathroom to take a shower. Inside the shower, Larry let the water run down his frustrated body. Not only had Brandy changed, but their sex life or lack of has changed. It was almost as if she can't stand for him to touch her anymore, and this made him believe she was sleeping with her boss.

One week later

Jarrod and Larry were on their lunch break when they pull into BP to get some deli sandwiches and some soda.

"So, how are things with you and Brandy?"

"Nothing's changed if anything, things are worse. I'm sleeping in the guest bedroom. She comes and goes as she pleases. I love her so much man, I just want her to love me as much as I love her."

"I still can't believe how's she's acting. I thought you two would have had a little one by now and another one on the way."

"Right! Hell, I doubt if she even wants any kids. The way I see things now, kids would just get in her way."

Later that day, Larry, Jarrod, and another co-worker were just about to close up shop. The co-worker had just pulled down the last bay door to the shop when out of nowhere a beautiful, sexy chocolate woman appeared frantically.

"Excuse me, sir, can you help me with my car?"

"Ma'am, I'm sorry, but we're closed," Terrance said.

"Sir, I will pay you whatever you want. I just need my flat fixed now, please."

"Ma'am, my hands are tied. We are closed."

Larry and Jarrod were discussing dinner plans when Larry overheard a conversation between the co-worker and a lady when he left Jarrod in mid-sentence. Larry stepped outside and as he did, he froze in his tracks. The woman before the worker stood about 5'7 with the prettiest Hershey colored skin that Larry had ever seen. As he moved closer, Larry was more intrigued by her. Her body language gave off confidence, her shapely legs caught his attention and when she turned around to see who was walking up behind her, Larry was hit with her beautiful smile.

"Miss, how can I help you, what seems to be the problem?" Larry asked.

"Oh my God! Thank you so much. I have a flat tire. I'm on my way to meet a client and if I'm late, I just might lose the biggest client I ever had and I cannot afford to lose any clients."

Larry looked back at Jarrod as he followed behind Miss sexual chocolate. Larry tried his best to keep his eyes straight ahead and not on her badunka dunk, but it was hard. She wore a short black skirt with a short white crop top that shows off her midsection and her pierced belly button. As she continued to walk in her six-inch stilettos, Larry looked at her chocolate defined legs as his eyes inched up to the middle of her thighs.

"Damn!"

Alex turned to look at Larry.

"Is something wrong?" Alex asked.

"Oh no, just thinking out loud."

Alex opened the car door, bent over, and grabbed her keys from the ignition. As she did, Larry got a full view of her cheeks along with her thong that covered the split between her ass and showed the thickness of her lips. Larry couldn't believe what he was witnessing, it was as if she was hypnotizing him with her body.

Alex turned and handed Larry the keys.

"Here you go. The spare tire is in the trunk."

Larry looked puzzled as a wave of dizziness came over him. He took a step back and took a deep breath.

"Are you okay?" Alex asked.

"Yeah, I'm Okay." Larry lied.

Larry walked to the back of the car to the trunk where he found the spare tire. He pulled the tire out of the trunk and walked back to the driver's side of the car. He was busy replacing the flat tire while Alex paced back and forth, exuding her female scent. Her smell was so intoxicating that Larry had a hard time focusing on the tire.

"So what side of town are you from?" Larry asked.

"I'm from the Northeast side."

"If you don't mind me asking, what brings you over here to the Southside of town?"

"I have a meeting with a very important client."

"What type of work do you do?"

"I'm in Public relations."

"I know someone interested in that field. So are you working with any celebrities?"

"No, not yet. I haven't made it big yet."

Larry tried his best to keep his eyes off her shapely thighs, but it was hard seeing that she continued to walk back and forth enticing him more each time, and then out of nowhere, she moved to stand right in front of him. Larry was afraid to look up because she was so close if he looked up, he would see right up her skirt.

The smell from her womanhood made him weak. He wanted to do more than change her tire.

Larry came to his senses and moved back, stood up and pulled a rag from his back pocket, and wiped his hands off.

"All done."

"Oh my God, you have no idea what you just did for me. You saved my ass. How much do I owe you?"

"You don't owe me anything."

"Are you sure?"

"Yes, go meet your client."

"Thank you so much, Larry!"

Larry walked back inside the shop where Jarrod stood watching.

"Damn, sexual chocolate got it going on. She bent over, giving a brotha a free look and everything. Man, her pussy lips were fat as hell."

"Well, did you get that number?" Jarrod asked.

"What number?"

"Come on, man, don't tell me you didn't get her phone number."

"And why would I do that?"

"Because she's hot ass hell and your girl is sleeping with her boss."

"I never said she was sleeping with him. What I said was I thought she was, there's a difference."

"You didn't have to."

"Can we just drop the subject," Larry said with frustration.

Larry locked the shop's front door and walked swiftly to his car. Larry and Jarrod rode separately to the District Tap. Larry was furious, but not with Jarrod, but with himself for allowing Brandy to take him through these changes.

Chapter Three

Jarrod and Larry stood waiting to be seated when his mind drifted back to the lady at the shop. He replayed the images in his head of her bending over. Larry tried to shake the images, but he couldn't. It was like his mind was a video camera that repeatedly played the images repeatedly.

"Oh my God!" Larry said aloud, trying to shake the images of Sexual Chocolate as he called her.

"Man, what's wrong with you?"

"Nothing." Larry shook his head.

"Hello and how are you guys doing this evening?" The waitress asked.

"We're good and you?"

"I'm great and thanks for asking. If you will follow me, I will get you guys seated."

"Man, I can't stop thinking about Alex."

"Alex, who the hell is that?"

Larry laughed, "Sexual Chocolate."

"Oh, so that's her name. Man, I told you, to get her number."

"Man, come on. Brandy and I are still married, no matter how bad things are right now."

"So why are you thinking about her then?"

"I don't know. It's like she put a spell on me. I cannot stop thinking about her and her smell, it's all up in my nostrils."

Jarrod laughed and shook his head, "If that had been me, relationship or not, I would have been all over that ass."

"Oh, I know you would have. You probably would have tried to fuck her in the shop."

After dinner, Larry and Jarrod walked out of the restaurant and stood outside talking before parting ways.

Brandy pulled into the driveway, cut the engine, and exited the car. She walked around her car to the walkway where she noticed a black sedan parked in front of their home. She couldn't see if anyone was inside because of the tinted windows.

Brandy walked in expecting to see a guest, but as she made her way to the living area, it was empty. She walked further down the hall to the den and then to the kitchen.

"Larry, where are you?" Brandy called out to him.

Brandy yelled throughout the house until Larry appeared at the top of the stairs.

"What is it?"

"Is someone up there with you?" Larry shook his head.

"And why would I have someone up here with me? Oh, let me guess. Since you're cheating, I guess I must be cheating. Or could it be that since you're not fucking me, I must be fucking someone else? Which one is it Brandy?"

"Larry, please I'm not accusing you of anything and I'm not trying to argue with you either."

"I know. You're not trying to do anything with me, are you?"

Larry walked back into the guest bedroom. He refused to sleep in the same bed with Brandy.

The next morning at work, Larry walked in, and all eyes were on him.

"What's up with you guys?"

"What's up with you, no I didn't get her number?"

"What are you talking about?" Larry asked.

Jarrod pointed to the fruit basket that had been delivered just before Larry walked in.

"What is this and who is it from?"

"Read the card."

Larry looked at the card.

"It's not what you think."

"So you mean to tell me that Ms. Sexual Chocolate is making all of this up?"

Larry continued to read the card: Larry, thank you so much for last night. I enjoyed every bit of you…. Alex.

"Whoa! What the hell is she talking about and what is she up too? I did not spend the night with her. I put her spare tire on for her and that's it. I don't even know how she knows my name because I didn't tell her."
Jarrod laughed.

"You can laugh all you want, but I'm telling you the truth."
Larry recalled the dream he had last night. In his dream, the lady from the shop came to him butt naked. Her chocolate skin glistened in the dark as the moon shined on her through the window. She kissed every inch of his body from his toes, making her way to his forehead, but not before taking him in her mouth. She ran her tongue around the top of his head and inserting it into her mouth. She licked this side of him with her tongues as if she was licking a Popsicle. It felt so good and real to him that he caught himself moaning and woke from the dream. He was moist and sticky.

"Larry, what's up with you?"
Jarrod laughed at Larry as he walked toward the back, shaking his head.

Chapter Four

That evening when Larry arrived home, Brandy greeted him just as he stepped foot inside the home.

"How dare you accuse me of sleeping with Benjamin when you're the one who's been cheating."

Brandy threw a small card at Larry as she dashed upstairs.

Larry read the card as he made his way further into the room where he spotted a dozen red roses. It had the same wording that the card at work had.

"What is up with this chick? Brandy, we need to talk."

"Larry, I'm not in the mood to talk."

"Brandy, we need to talk!" Larry shouted.

"Leave me alone, Larry!"

Larry gave up and made his way to the guest bedroom. He turned the television on and flicked through the channels, but he couldn't find anything to take his mind off his problems. He reached over and grabbed his phone off the nightstand and dialed Jarrod's number.

"What's up, man?"

"Nothing. Just chillin. What's up with you?"

"Bored as hell. Hey, let's go out and have a drink or two," Larry said.

Larry and Jarrod met at Scotty's Brewhouse on 96th street.

"Man, you are not going to believe what was waiting for me when I got home."

"Spill it," Jarrod said anxiously.

A dozen red roses with the same damn card that was attached to the fruit basket at work. Brandy was shitty as hell.

"Man, be honest, it's me you're talking to. You swear you didn't smash ole girl."

"Jarrod, how many years have you known me and how many times have you known me to cheat on a woman?"

"Okay, you got me there, but what is up with this woman?"

"I have no idea."

An hour later, Larry and Jarrod were ready to leave and was getting ready to pay their bill.

"Oh, I forgot to tell you guys, another patron paid your bill." The waiter told them.

Larry and Jarrod looked at each other.

"I don't even want to know who," Larry shook his head.

Outside of Scotty's

"Man, I'll see you tomorrow, but do me a favor and be careful," Jarrod told Larry as the two shook hands and walked in the opposite direction to their cars. Once Larry was inside his car, he put the key in the ignition and tried to start it, but it would not turn over. Larry got out, popped the hood and worked under the hood and when he couldn't figure out what was wrong, he closed the hood, and when he did, he found Alex sitting in the driver's seat of his car.

"What the fuck!"

Larry walked over to the driver's side of his car and opened the door.

"What are you doing in my car?"

"Is that any way to treat someone who sexed you good last night?"

"What! You have lost your damn mind. Don't you know I am married, and my wife saw your little gift and the card.

"I'm just kidding, so don't go getting your drawls all in a knot. And as far as your wife, if she was taking care of you you wouldn't have anything to worry about. Anyway, my car won't start so I need a ride home."

"Why didn't you call an Uber?"

"Because I figured a nice man like yourself would give a helpless woman like me a ride home."

Alex got out of the car and walked around to the passenger side and got in. Larry looked at her sideways.

"You are bold as hell," Larry said as he got behind the wheel and turned the ignition and to his surprise, it turned over on the first try.

"Unbelievable."

"What's unbelievable?" Alex asked.

"Nothing, where am I taking you?"

Alex rattled off her address.

On the ride home, Larry found himself so intrigued by Alex. He caught himself eyeing her chocolate thighs, moving his eyes up to her perky breasts.

"You see something you like?"

"No." Larry laughed as he tried to keep his focus on the road and his mind off of Alex.

"Was that your black sedan parked on the side of the restaurant?"

"Yes."

"What's wrong with it now?"

"I don't know. I may need a new alternator. I'll have my brother Benny, bring me back to get it in the morning."

"Are you the one that paid our bill back at Scotty's?"

"What do you think?"

"What is it you want with me, Alex?"

"What makes you think I want something from you?"

"You show up out of nowhere and now you have my wife and my coworkers thinking I'm sleeping with you."

"I'm just looking for a friend. Is that so bad?"

Alex placed her hand on Larry's thigh. Larry looked over at her and moved her hand and placed it back on her lap.

Alex grabbed hold of his hand before he moved it.

Larry pulled into the driveway of a house that looked like a cottage from a fairy tale. It looked creepy.

"Is this it?"

"Yes, it is, home sweet home. Would you like to come in for a minute?"

"No, it's late. I should get home."

"Well, can you at least walk me to the door?"

Larry went against his better judgment and walked Alex to her front door.

"Now, did that kill you?" Alex said as she grabbed hold of his hand. Alex moved to stand directly in front of Larry. She was so close that Larry felt her heart beating. Her smell was so intoxicating that he almost choked.

"How about dinner tomorrow evening? It's my treat. I want to treat you for being such a gentleman?" Alex asked as she ran her hand up and then down his chest.

"I appreciate the offer, but you know I can't do that, Alex."

"The offer still stands if you change your mind."

"Woman, go on inside so I can get out of here."

Larry stood as Alex unlocked her front door and waited until she was safely inside. He stood there as it rained, thinking about her smooth chocolate skin, the smell of her body scent, and her voluptuous ass.

The sound of thunder brought him back to his senses. He rushed back to his car and was on his way home.

Denise Hill- The Seed

Chapter Five

That night, Larry tossed and turned most of the night, until sleep fell upon him. He was in a deep sleep when he felt aroused. He felt the lips of someone wrapped around his manhood. He enjoyed the feel of plump lips moving up and down him and when she climbed on top of him and rode him; it was like heaven to him, the feeling was so intense, but he was enjoying every bit and when it was over, it petrified him at what he saw. He saw a monster dressed in red with horns and a long tail. Larry was so afraid that he fell out of bed and was fighting with his sheets and yelling when Brandy burst into his room.

"Get away from me!" Larry yelled. Larry looked up and saw Brandy standing there. He felt like a complete idiot.

"What the hell are you doing?" Brandy asked.

"What do you want?"

"I came in here because I heard you yelling. I thought someone was in here hurting you," Brandy said with an attitude.

"Well, as you can see, I'm fine," Larry said embarrassed. Brandy looked at him and rolled her eyes.

"Can you please keep the noise down? I do have to work in the morning."

Larry sat up against the wall. It puzzled him. His penis was sore and moist from cum.

The next morning, Larry awakened sitting in the same spot up against the wall.

"Damn, what is going on with me?"

It exhausted Larry. He felt like he was coming down with a cold or something.

Larry arrived to work and ran into Jarrod. "Damn man, what's up with you. You don't look so good," Jarrod said.

"I know and I feel like shit."

30

Larry was still dragging by the afternoon and he just couldnn't get himself together. His boss told him to take the rest of the day off and get some rest. He looked and felt horrible.

Larry headed upstairs to the guest bedroom. He removed his shoes and flopped down on the bed. He stacked his pillows up and lay his head down, turned the TV on, and flicked through the channels. He tried to find something to take his mind off of Alex, but so far, nothing had worked.

Larry dozed off and dreamt about the lady that had been haunting him in his dreams. She came to him in a red form-fitting crotchless onesie. She unfastened his pants and pulled his penis out. She licked the tip and circled the head with her tongue until Larry became long and hard. Then she straddled him and slowly sat down onto him. The wetness and tightness of her pussy felt good. She raised up and slowly lowered herself back down and then continued until the feeling took over. She rode Larry faster and faster. Larry moaned and groaned. He felt his toes curl from the feeling and before he came; she removed herself, placed her pussy in his face, and took him in her mouth. She licked him from side to side around his head before making him disappear in her mouth. Larry licked her pussy from the crack of her ass to the front of her pussy. Her taste and smell had him high. The more he ate of her, the more he craved her. Then suddenly, she placed herself back onto his dick and rode him until they exploded with pleasure. Larry finally opened his eyes to get a look at her, and what he saw frightened the hell out of him. He was so afraid that he couldn't move, all he could do was look. He watched the monster face woman walk toward the door. The more he looked, the longer her tail became until she vanished.

Larry felt paralyzed. Then all at once, Larry awakened from the worst best dream he had ever had. He looked around the room and everything seemed normal, but when he looked down at his pants, his pants were down around

his ankles and his penis was out. Larry jumped up and ran
to his bedroom door.

"Brandy, Brandy, is that you?" Larry called out.

Larry assumed it had been Brandy that had just seduced
him. Minutes later, he removed his clothes and walked
down the hall to the bathroom naked. As he entered the
shower, he got a strange feeling that someone was watching
him. He got a cold chilled that ran down his body. Larry
looked around the shower and listened before turning the
water on. He half expected to see Brandy jump out at him
at any minute, but to his surprise or disappointment, that
did not happen.

Larry turned the water on, stood under the spray as the
warm water ran down his body. His mind returned to his
dream. The dream felt so real and from the dampness of his
penis he knew he did not dream this, but what he couldn't
understand is why he continued to have this dream. Just as
Larry finished showering, he heard the bathroom door shut.

"Brandy, is that you?"

Larry didn't get an answer, so he grabbed a towel, wrapped
it around his body, and exited the bathroom.

"Who's there?"

Larry made his way down the hall to their bedroom. He
slowly opened the door, hoping to see Brandy. He made his
way further into the room looking around suspiciously and
out of nowhere, he saw a shadow run past the bedroom
door. Larry took off out the door.

"Hey, who's there? I have a gun, so whoever you are,
you need to come out with your hands up."

Larry saw something red, right in front of his bedroom
door. Now he knew someone was trying to mess with his
mind because this was not there before. Larry walked over,
bent down, and picked up the onesie. The smell from the
onesie is the same smell he had been smelling for the last
couple of days. He's even smelled this in his dream while
the monster was sexing him. Larry held the onesie to his

nose. The smell was so intoxicating and out of nowhere; he heard a voice.

"Go ahead and take in the aroma of my bodily scent."
Larry stood there frozen. He couldn't move or speak. It was like he was in a trance. In the meantime, Brandy made her way upstairs. She came home early to pack because she and her boss, Benjamin, were going away for a few days on a business trip.

"What is up with you? You're just standing there looking like you just seen a ghost or something," Brandy asked.
Larry stood there, still in shock as Brandy entered the bedroom to pack her overnight bag.
Minutes later, Larry stood in the doorway.

"And where the hell do you think you're going?"

"Larry, don't start with me. I have a business trip to go on. I will only be gone for a few days."

"And why am I just now hearing about this?"

"It was a last-minute decision. Ben just told me."

"Oh, so it's Ben now. And why do you think I'm going to allow my wife to go on a business trip with her boss, or should I say, her lover?"

"See, this is why I can't tell you anything. You always take things the wrong way."

"The wrong way. Is there a right way to tell your husband at the last damn minute you're going on an overnight trip with a man you've been spending so much time with that your husband thinks you're having an affair with him? Is there?"

"Larry, nothing is going on between us. I wish you would believe me. It's just business, I promise."

"And what happens if I tell you I don't want you to go? If it's just business, he can have your other co-worker go. The one that's not married. Oh, my bad, I forgot, she's fat as hell and unattractive."

"Larry, it is just business and whether you like it or not, I'm going. This is my career we're talking about here. This could be a big step in the right direction for me. I can meet some very important people at this business meeting. This is the only reason Ben asked me to attend. He's trying to help me with my career."

"Help you with your career. Ha! I just bet he is. The only thing I see him helping you with is to destroy your marriage. Do you value this marriage any more Brandy?"

"Now you're being ridiculous. You know damn well I value our marriage, and Ben is not trying to destroy our marriage. You know you could learn a lot from him."
Larry looked at his wife and shook his head.

"You're comical, I see. Why don't you show me how much you value this marriage by not going on this trip?"

"Larry, I can't do that, but what I can do is when I get back we will take a much-needed vacation and focus on us."

"Like hell, we will. If you leave, don't bother coming back Brandy and I mean that."
Brandy reached up to kiss Larry, but he turned away.
Larry stood at the top of the stairs looking down at Brandy.

"Larry, please understand. We will talk when I return. I love you!"

Denise Hill- The Seed

Chapter Six

Larry couldn't believe his wife chose her boss over him. The offer that Alex made to him sounded more and more appealing, he thought. Larry was still wrapped in his towel and went into his bedroom, grabbed his phone and dialed Alex, and just as she picked up, he hung up.

"Shit! What am I doing?"

Alex grabbed her phone on the first ring. She knew it was Larry by the ringtone she stored in her phone earlier that day.

"Larry," Alex laughed as she heard the dial tone. Alex quickly dialed Larry back.

"Hello."

"Oh, so you just gonna hang up on me."

"I'm sorry, Alex. I shouldn't have called you."

"And why not? Tell me one good reason and I don't want to hear I'm married because we both know how that is."

"What are you talking about? And who have you been talking to?"

"I haven't talked to anyone. It's written all over your face. There's so much sadness in your eyes. I want to replace it with happiness."

Larry only wished Brandy cared about him as much as Alex seemed to right now. He could feel the warmness from Alex through the phone and it felt good.

"Does your dinner offer still stand?"

"For you, always," Alex said, smiling.

Larry arrived at Alex's. He wanted to meet her at the restaurant, but her car was in the shop, so he agreed to pick her up since she was treating him to dinner. Larry walked to the front door. He paused for a minute. He felt an uneasiness come over him. He knew he had to be strong unless he would find himself in bed with Alex.

Just as he was about to knock, the door opened.

"Are you just going to stand there?"

Alex said as she laughed at Larry. Larry stood there with a look of horror on his face when Alex opened the door.

"I didn't expect you to snatch the door open so fast."

"Come on in while I finish getting ready. Have a seat and make yourself at home." Alex walked back to her room to finish getting dressed.

"There are drinks in the fridge if you want something to drink," Alex yelled from the bedroom.

"Something cold sounds good right about now," Larry said as he made his way to the kitchen. When he returned, Alex was standing there in a tight-fitting red dress with black stilettos.

"Damn you look good."

Larry couldn't keep his eyes off of her as he made his way to stand in front of her.

Alex moved closer to Larry. Her smell igniting from her body was the same smell Larry smelled earlier in his home.

"It can't be."

"What can't be?"

"Your perfume. I smelled this in my home earlier today."

"Does your wife where this scent?"

"I'm not sure. You know if you're not careful I just might kiss you," Larry said as his hand moved to Alex's face and traced her lips with his finger.

"If you're not careful, I just might let you while I'm fucking you with my words."

"Oh, really. I've never had anyone fuck me with their words."

"You should try it sometimes, you just might like it."

The two stood there for a minute or two, tonguing each

other down and moaning as the feeling took over. The bulge in Larry's pants let him know what time it was. Larry broke the kiss as he breathed deeply, "Alex, I want you so bad, but I can't do this to Brandy. I agreed to dinner, and that's it. So let's get out of here while I can."

"How do you know your wife's not cheating on you?"Alex asked as she plants little kisses to Larry's face and as her hand massaged the bulge in his pants.

"Shh... Don't say a word."
Alex stopped the kisses and the massage. Alex whispered into Larry's ear as her warm breath breathed deep in his ear.

"Listen to the sound of my voice and relax, let your mind go as I fuck you with my words and with your imagination. Can you feel the warmth of my tongue on your dick as I lick around your head and your pre cum seeps out? Do you like the feel of my tongue sliding up and down the side of your dick as my hand massages your balls? Do you like the feel of my mouth as I take you in and deep throat you? Are you throbbing and waiting anxiously to enter my wet, tight, juicy pussy? Do you want me as bad as I want you? How long will you wait to take me? Can you imagine turning me over, removing my thong, and eating me out from my ass to my pussy? Does it excite you when you move your dick all around my pussy before entering my ass and then my pussy? Do you feel me like I feel you? It feels so damn good, Larry. I want you to fuck me harder, go deeper and deeper until you touch my soul. Aw baby, don't stop. Can you feel me tightening up around your dick? Does it feel good to you? Talk to me, baby."

"Oh yes! Your pussy is tight, just like I like. Please, Alex, give it to me, give it all to me. Aw shit! Fuck me baby, fuck the hell out of me. Oh shit, aw hell!" Larry screamed as he came. Minutes later when his breathing was back to normal. He stood there in awe. He couldn't believe he was just fucked and fucked real good without ever being touched.

"Damn, what the fuck did you just do to me."
Alex laughed as she led him down the hallway to the bathroom.

"There's a clean washcloth on the counter."
When he returned to the room, Alex was sitting on the couch.

"So are you relaxed now?"

"Yes, very," Larry laughed.

"I want to make a quick stop by my house to change if you don't mind."

"No, not at all."

At Larry's home

"You can have a seat I will be right back."
Larry ran upstairs to his bedroom and then the bathroom to freshen up and changed his underwear and jeans.
In the meantime, Alex made her way around his living room and den, checking out everything. She walked over and picked up a picture of Larry and Brandy. She ran her hand across Larry's face before she slid the picture into her purse.

"Are you ready?"
Alex jumped at the sound of his voice.

"Yes, I am. I am starved."

Denise Hill- The Seed

Chapter Seven

Larry and Alex were eating, laughing, and enjoying each other's company when Larry looked up and saw Brandy and Benjamin walk pass the restaurant.

"What the fuck!" Larry yelled, and some patron's looked his way.

"What's wrong?"

"I can't believe this. Wait here, I'll be right back."

Larry rushed outside, but by the time he made it out there, they were nowhere in sight. Larry stood there in silence, looking puzzled. He knew there was no way they could have disappeared that quickly, and he knew he saw them. Larry walked back inside and took his seat. Right now he was so confused.

"Are you going to tell me what's going on?"

"I thought I saw my wife and her boss walking together hand in hand."

"Really. I thought she was out of town on a business trip?"

"Who told you that?"

"You did."

"No, I never mentioned that to you."

"How forgetful are we? So what happened when you went outside?"

"They were nowhere in sight."

"Um..."

Alex sat with a smirk on her face. While Larry looked at her trying to figure out how Alex knew about Brandy's business trip.

"Can we get out of here?"

"Sure."

Alex flagged the waiter over and paid their bill.

Larry and Alex walked along the canal. The moon was shining, and the wind blew a nice warm breeze, and the scenery was perfect.

"God, this is so perfect. I love the summer. I love doing things like this, but lately, I haven't been able to enjoy these things with my wife. I wish she could be more like you. You seem so understanding and you're so easy to talk to."

"Because she's not me. She's all about herself and what she wants. Has she always been this way?"

"No, not in the beginning. I first noticed a change when her old boss was murdered and they hired a new guy to replace him. It appeared as though the new guy was just waiting in the wind for something like this to happen because he stepped right in and no one had ever heard of him before. I believe she's having an affair with him."

"Oh, I'm sorry to hear that, but what are you going to do about it?"

"What can I do. I love her to death." Larry said as he turned to face Alex. I can't just turn my feelings off and on whenever I want.

It floored Alex. She cannot believe what she was hearing.

"What! Wait a minute. Are you telling me you will not do anything even though you think your wife is sleeping with her boss?"

Alex stopped walking. She turned to face Larry.

"You know you deserve better than that, right? Larry, you are one of a kind. You're handsome, loving and a devoted husband. You should demand the same from your mate and if you don't get the same, you shouldn't be in that marriage."

"Alex, I appreciate your kind words, but it's not that easy to just leave someone that you care about. I'm in love with Brandy. I have never stepped out on her, besides the time I kissed you, and forgive me for saying this, but it is the truth. I only kissed you because I was lonely and I missed the intimacy I share with Brandy."

"Oh, really! You know what, you deserve everything you get. You wouldn't know a good woman if you had one. You're no different from these other weak men."

Larry stood there in shock. He couldn't believe the things that Alex just said. Am I weak, he wondered?

"So you think I'm weak for staying with someone that I love."

"Pretty much."

"And why is that? Is it because I stayed with someone who doesn't treat me the way I treat her? Marriage is not something that you take lightly, you can't just end your marriage without trying to work it out first."

"Yes, and because you think she's sleeping with her boss and you have done nothing about it. I know there will always be problems in marriages, but if you're the only one trying to make it work, it will not work, so stop wasting your time and move the fuck on!"

"Everyone Handles things differently. Just because I have done nothing, doesn't mean I won't handle the situation and I won't stay in this marriage if we can't work things out."

"Um… Whatever." Alex rolled her eye.

"Can we just change the subject?"

"What do you do in your spare time? Alex asked."

"Not much of anything. My boy and I hang out from time to time."

"What is it you want to do with your life?" Alex asked as she looked up at Larry.

"I want to travel the world. Have two kids and just enjoy my family. What is it you want to do?"

"I want to get married and have about three or four kids."

Larry looked at his watch, "I should get you home."

Larry pulled into Alex's driveway. He cut the engine, and the two sat in silence. Larry lay his head back on the headrest.

"Are you tired?"

"Yes, I'm exhausted."

"You can crash at my place. I have an extra room."

"I appreciate it, but I can't. Let me walk you to your door."

Larry walked over to the passenger side and opened the door for Alex.

"You are such a gentleman."

"I know."

Alex and Larry walked up the walkway to her front door.

"Are you sure you won't stay? I promise to keep my hands and my thoughts to myself."

Larry chuckled.

"Naw, it wouldn't look good on my part to spend the night with a woman when I know I'm a married man."

"Are you serious? Never mind, I'll keep my thoughts to myself."

Larry stood there admiring Alex as the rain fell. He loved the way her lip turned up when she talked. He loved her creamy chocolate skin and her smell drove him crazy. The feeling that stirred up inside told him one thing and that was if he didn't leave right then, he will end up sleeping with her.

"Good night," Alex.

Larry ran to his car.

Alex walked inside and stood at the front door and then moved to the window where she stood staring out into the darkness, pacing back and forth.

Larry got in his car and when he turned the ignition, it didn't turn over. Larry tried several times, but with his luck, he was stuck at Alex's. Larry got out and ran to the front door, but hesitated before knocking. Torn between right and wrong, something pulled at him to do wrong. He stood there drenched from the pouring rain and suddenly he moved toward the door to knock, but the front door opened.

"Oh my God, you're soaked. Well, don't just stand there silly, come on in and get out of the rain and out of those wet clothes."

Larry walked slowly inside in disarray.

"Look at you."

Alex removed his shirt and started unbutton his belt.

"I got this."

Larry removed Alex's hand from his belt buckle.

'You are going to catch a cold if you don't get out of those wet pants."

Larry handed Alex his shirt. She went and got a towel so he could dry off.

"I'll put your clothes in the dryer."

"Okay, but in the meantime, I will call Jarrod."

Larry tried to dial out, but he could not get a signal. He continued to move around the room, trying to get a signal.

"Hey, can I use your phone? I can't seem to get a signal."

"Sure."

Alex handed Larry her phone. Larry tried several times to get a signal.

"Do you ever have problems getting signals inside your home?"

"No, I've never had a problem until now."

After Larry's clothes dried, he tried to get a signal outside but was unsuccessful.

"Damn," Larry said. It frustrated him that he couldn't get a signal.

Alex walked up to Larry.

"I told you, you're welcome to crash here and in the morning if you can't get your car started, I will go over to the neighbors to use their phone to call someone from your shop to come over and look at it."

Larry looked at Alex.

"I promise I will be a good girl," Alex said.

"What other choice do I have besides walking 50 miles home in the pouring rain."

Larry knew this was a bad idea, but what could he do, but be on his best behavior. He followed as Alex escorted him to her guest bedroom. Inside, Larry undressed down to his boxers and wife beater and climbed underneath the covers. Alex stood outside the door for a minute before heading to her room.

Denise Hill- The Seed

Chapter Eight

Larry fought the feeling of someone's lips as she kissed him passionately on the lips and slowly made her way down his chest where she took his nipple into her mouth. She sucked on it until it became hard. She then moved down south as she planted kisses to his stomach before reaching his manhood. Once she was there, she grabbed the base of his penis while her tongue circled the head before taking him in.

Larry moaned loudly that he awakened himself up from the dream he was having and when he opened his eyes, Alex was standing at the foot of the bed. Larry jumped when he saw Alex standing there in a red sheer nightgown. He pulled the cover over him, trying to hide his hard-on.

"I heard you from my room. You must have had some dream. Are you okay? Can I get you something to drink?"

"No, I'm fine."

It puzzled Larry. He couldn't believe he was dreaming about this lady again, and then to find Alex standing at the foot of the bed when he awoke. This was some weird shit.

"Well, if you need anything, my room is upstairs to the left. You better get some rest."

Alex turned to leave with a wicked smile on her face, but just then, Larry called out to her.

"Alex!" Alex turned around and looked at Larry.

"I need you."

Alex slowly walked toward Larry as she removed the straps of her nightgown and allowed her gown to slide down her body. Once she reached the bed, Larry looked at her smooth creamy skin. He moved closer as he allowed his tongue to slide up her midsection to the center of her breast. He then took his tongue and ran it across her nipple before taking it in his mouth. He licked and sucked until it becomes hard, then he took more of her breast in his mouth

48

as his hand found its way down to her womanhood. He slowly unfolded her thick pussy lips to find her treasure. He allowed his finger to rub her clit until it became hard. He moved down to her vagina where he inserted his two fingers. He moved in and out and back to her clit repeatedly until she couldn't take much more.

"Oh, Poppy I want you to fuck me."
Alex said with a Spanish accent.
Larry pulled Alex down onto the bed and bury's himself between her legs. He went to town as he licked her from her pussy to her ass.

"Larry, please, I need you inside me now!"
Larry rose up and looked at Alex.

"So you want this right here?"
He asked as he ran his penis up and down her pussy.

"Yes!"

"How bad do you want this?"
Larry asked as he slid the head in and back out.

"Aw baby, you're wet, juicy, and hot just like I like."
Larry slid in and pulled out slowly.

"Aw shit. You feel so damn good, baby."

"Stop playing with me, Larry, and fuck me!" Alex yelled.
Larry slid back in and moved deeper and faster. He raised Alex's legs over his shoulder. He wanted to go as deep as he could. The feeling was so overwhelming that he almost shit on himself, or at least this was how he felt. As he came, he got a glimpse of the monster lady as he looked at Alex.

"Damn, what the fuck!"
Larry yelled as he released himself. Larry felt sick, exhausted, and his dick became even more sore. He lay next to Alex in bed just laying there staring at the ceiling. He lay awake for hours trying to decide if he was really fucking Alex or the monster lady. Now he wondered who Alex was. Larry looked over at Alex as she lay asleep next to him and images of the monster lady appeared again.

That morning, Larry awoke to the smell of coffee brewing, bacon, eggs, and toast. Larry threw the covers off, grabbed his shirt, pants, and put his shoes on. He opened the door to the bedroom and walked down the hall.

Larry made his way into the kitchen where he found Alex slaying away and all at once, his stomach felt like it was knotting up.

Larry took off down the hall to the bathroom where he vomited. When he finished, he sat down on the floor and rested his back against the tub.

Alex walked down the hall to the restroom to see if Larry was okay. Alex stuck her head inside the bathroom where she found Larry on the floor sitting.

"Good morning," Larry said.

"Good morning. Are you okay and how did you sleep?"

"Not good and not good. I'm so glad I'm off today."

Alex helped Larry up. He walked over to the sink and turned to face her.

"Do you have an extra toothbrush and washcloth?"

Alex walked over to the linen closet and pulled out a toothbrush, towel, and washcloth.

"When you're ready, meet me in the kitchen."

"Okay, thanks."

Larry brushed his teeth and washed his face. He looked at his image in the mirror.

"Damn, I look just like how I feel. Like shit!"

He lay the toothbrush and washcloth on the corner of the sink and made his way back down the hall to the kitchen.

"Have a seat and I will fix you a plate."

"First, let me try to start my car again."

Larry walked outside to his car. He unlocked the door, got behind the wheel, and put the key in the ignition and it started right up. Larry cut the engine and restarted the car and again, and it started right up again.

"Um… this is too strange."

Larry scratched his head and then pulled out his phone, and he got a strong signal.

"This is some crazy shit."

Larry walked back inside the house, looking strangely at Alex.

"Well, did it start?"

"Right up and I have a signal on the phone too."

"Um... that's strange."

"Yeah. Everything about last night was strange."

"What do you mean everything about last night is strange?"

Larry thought back to his dream or nightmare. He now realized Alex and the monster lady are the same people.

"Who and what are you, Alex?"

"What do you mean? Are you okay?"

"No, not really. I don't know what it is, but I don't feel like myself and I feel like you're not who you say you are. Where did you come from and what do you want with me?"

"I'm not sure what you're talking about, Larry. I was born and raised here in Indiana and as I told you before, I want to be your friend."

Larry squinted his eyes at Alex.

"I'm serious. I need to know who and what you are and what do you want with me?"

"What did I just say?"

"Well, I'm going to head over to the ER."

"Are you serious?"

"Yes."

"Do you want me to come with you?"

"Naw, I'm good."

Alex walked over to Larry and grabbed a hold of his pants and pulled him close to her. She reached for his belt and tried to unfasten it, but Larry stopped her.

"Come on Larry, you will enjoy this."

Alex unfastened Larry's pants and unzipped the zipper and pulled his penis out. She put him in her mouth. The feeling that went through Larry's body was amazing. Alex removed him from her mouth and guided him to the couch where she instructed him to lie down. She pulled his pants down to his ankles and straddled him. She inserted him inside of her and gave him the ride of his life. The feeling was so overwhelming it was nothing like he had ever felt before, and all at once, he couldn't move or talk. He can only feel the walls of Alex's pussy wrapped around him. Alex continued to ride him. His penis was so sore, but the feeling he felt was so powerful. He tried to scream and to tell Alex to stop, but he couldn't speak, his body was paralyzed so he lay there enjoying the most precious feeling, but it also pained him. Once they both came, Alex removed herself and made her way into the bathroom.

Alex looked at herself in the mirror and smiled, and rubbed her stomach. She did a happy dance. "You're almost complete, my little one," Alex said.

Larry lay there unable to move as the tears rolled down the side of his face from the pain that he was in.

Alex walked back into the living room and walked over and stood over Larry.

"Aw, what's the matter honey cat got your tongue."

Alex laughed as she walked away.

Larry continued to lay wondering what the hell was wrong with him when his body tingled all over. He tried to move his arm, and he could move it a little. He tried again, and now he had full control of his movements. Larry got up slowly and bent down to pull up his boxers and his pants. He was out of the house and in his car in no time.

Denise Hill- The Seed

Chapter Nine

Later that afternoon, Larry went to the ER.

Larry was in the examining room waiting for the doctor to come back with some test results.

Larry heard a couple of nurses outside the room talking, and then the doctor entered with the two nurses by his side. The doctor walked over to Larry with his chart.

"Son, I'm not sure what's going on, but whatever it is, it's not good. Your organs are deteriorating."

"What are you talking about?"

"Your organs are not working properly, but we cannot understand why not. Hopefully, the test results that we get back next week will help us figure out what's going on with your body. I would say if you're a praying man, start praying because this doesn't look good."

Larry left the ER. He drove around for hours trying to figure out what was going on with him and Alex. He decided to visit his pastor for prayer and some advice.

Larry pulled into the pastor's driveway.

"Thank God he is home."

Larry got out of the car and walked up the walkway.

The pastor's housekeeper led Larry to the study where the pastor was.

"Well, look what the cat drug in. Praise the Lord, my son."

Larry walked further into the study. The pastor stood up behind his desk and moved to stand in front of his desk to greet Larry.

"Praise the Lord, Pastor."

The two men embraced each other, it shocked the pastor by the way Larry looked.

"Let's have a seat over here on the couch. Can Maria get you anything to drink or to eat?"

"No, I'm good."

"Are you sure because you don't look so good, son?"
Larry was a little hesitant to tell the pastor what was going on, but he knew if anyone can help him, the pastor could.

"Pastor, I have a problem that I need your help with."

"Is everything okay with you and Brandy?"

"No. I think she's having an affair with her boss."
The pastor ran his hand down the side of his face.

"How long has this been going on?"

"I'm not sure. I know she's been acting distant for about two months now. She won't even let me touch her and she spends a lot of time with her new boss now."

"Her new boss?"

"Yeah, her old boss was murdered in their parking garage."

"Um... Have you confronted her about this?"

"Yes, and she tells me it's not what I think and that it's all about business. Right now as we speak, she's on a business trip with him. But I could have sworn I had seen them together last night."

"And you allowed her to go?"

"No, I didn't allow her to do anything. She's a grown woman, but I told her if she left not to come back."

"Did you mean that?"

"Yes, at the time I did, but that's not why I'm here."
Larry struggled to get it out.

"Take your time, son."

"A week ago, a young lady came to the shop needing help with her flat tire, and being the man that I am, I helped her and now, I cannot get rid of her. The next day she sent me a fruit basket to the shop and roses to my home. Brandy read the note attached, so she thinks I'm sleeping with her."

"Well, are you?"
The pastor looked directly at Larry.
Larry thought about what he was going to say before saying it.

"No, not at first, but I've been having nightmares about

a sexy chocolate woman sexing me in my sleep and when I wake, my penis is damp. I feel so exhausted and my penis is so sore afterward. Each time I see this lady's face, it's the face of a monster. Last night I had sex with the young lady from the shop, and I think she's the monster that has been sexing me in my sleep. My health has started to deteriorate. I just left the ER where they ran several tests, but they're not sure what's going on. I'm scared right now. I can't keep anything on my stomach, I stay cold. I just feel horrible and it all started with my first nightmare."

The pastor sat further back on the couch.

"I would say you're having sex with an alien or demon, something not from this earth, and the alien or demon is the young lady from the shop. Don't you know that when an alien or demon has sex with men in their sleep often, their health deteriorates and could cause death? An Alien can take the form of any person and live out its lustful ways. I would bet any money on it that this thing is trying to get pregnant."

Larry sat stunned. He could not believe what he was hearing.

"Oh my God!"

Larry put both hands up to his face.

"How can I get rid of her?"

"I'm not sure, but whatever you do, don't have any contact with her until I figure out what we can do.'"

"I need to know how do I keep her from sexing me in my sleep. I'm not trying to die."

"Larry, your mind is probably all over the place. Your vulnerable because of the issues with you and Brandy. Keep your mind clean and free of this young lady and most of all stay prayed up. You're allowing her to enter through your dreams."

The pastor stood.

"Let's pray."

The pastor grabbed a hold of Larry's hand as they both bowed their heads. "Father in the name of Jesus. We are coming to you to ask for protection for Larry. We need you to send down his guardian angels to protect him from any evil spirits that are forcing their way upon him. We ask that you give him a clean heart, mind, and soul and that you put up a hedge of protection around him and keep him covered by the blood of Jesus Christ. We ask that you keep your hands wrapped around him tightly. I pray that you guide him in how you want him to go. I ask you in the name of Jesus to bless his marriage and that he and his wife work things out. I ask all these things in your wonderful name Amen."

Denise Hill- The Seed

Chapter Ten

After speaking with the pastor, Larry headed over to talk with Jarrod.

"On my God! I cannot believe this is happening to you. You know, back in college, we had to do a project on this, and let me tell you, that was some scary shit. Let me call some guys that were on my team for the project and see if they remember how to get rid of it."

"Man, I don't even want to go home or be alone. The Pastor said I have to keep my mind clear of Alex."

"You know you can stay here as long as you like."

"I appreciate it, man, but I don't want to bring this mess into your home."

"Man, I wish she would try to come over here."
Jarrod does some karate moves that he doesn't know.
Larry laughed, "Man, you're stupid. Just let me crash for a couple of hours in your spare bedroom."

Larry was so exhausted that he slept twelve hours straight. When he awoke, he was not sure where he was. He looked around at his surroundings until he realized he was still at Jarrod's. Larry lay there for twenty minutes before falling back to sleep.

Larry awoke again, but this time he was hungry. He cooked breakfast for Jarrod and himself.

Larry was busy in the kitchen when Jarrod walked in.

"Good morning. I see someone is feeling better."

"No, I'm not feeling much better, I'm just hungry. I hope I can keep this down."

"How did you sleep?"

"I slept well. No dreams, or should I say no one sexed me."

"So does Brandy know anything about this?"

"No. Why?"

"Don't you think she should know since this has been going on in your home?"

"Um, I never thought about it. I guess you right she should know whether she cares, but she has to be there for me to tell her."

After breakfast, Jarrod and Larry sat in the livingroom watching TV. Jarrod flicked through the channels until he came across Love and Basketball.

"Aw man, this is one of my favorite movies. I love me some Sanaa Lathan."

"Yeah, she is hot."

Larry made himself comfortable on the couch.

Two hours later, after the movie was over, Jarrod looked over at Larry, who was asleep. Jarrod couldn't understand why Larry was so tired. Jarrod reached over and nudged Larry on the knee.

"Are you okay, man?"

"Yeah, what time is it?"

Larry looked around the room.

"It's a little after one."

"I guess it's about time I get myself home. Thanks for letting me crash here last night. I appreciate it."

"No problem. Anytime."

Jarrod and Larry embraced each other.

Larry pulled into his driveway along the side of Brandy's car. He cut the engine and exited the car. He was so shocked to see Brandy's car that he never noticed the black sedan parked in front of the house.

Larry rushed up the walkway, pulled out his key, inserted it into the lock, and turned the knob slowly. As soon as Larry stepped inside, he heard a familiar voice coming from the den.

Larry moved further into the room until he was at the entry of the den. Brandy looked up and ran to Larry and kissed him on the lips.

"Alex, I would like you to meet my husband. The man I have neglected for months trying to get this business up and running. Larry, this is my new business partner, Alex."
Larry looked at Alex was so much hatred.

"Brandy, you need to get her the hell out of here right now!" Larry yelled!
Brandy grabbed a hold of Larry's arm and dragged him into the foyer.

"What the hell is wrong with you?"

"There are some things I need to tell you about your so-called business partner."
Just then, Alex walked out of the den, "You need to leave right now."

"I'm sorry Alex, I don't know what has come over my husband, but we will have to reschedule our meeting."
Alex slowly walked past Larry.

"Well, while you're telling her about me, make sure you tell her about Friday night."
Larry lunged out at Alex, but Brandy grabbed him.

"Larry, what is up with you?"
Suddenly, Larry felt sick to his stomach and rushed upstairs to the bathroom. Brandy was right behind him, but he shut the door in her face.

"Larry, what's wrong?"
Brandy stood outside the bathroom listening to Larry vomit.

"Larry, are you okay?"
Minutes later, Larry sat up against the bathtub. He felt weak and lightheaded.

"Brandy, can you call Jarrod and Pastor Simmons and have them come over here ASAP?"
Brandy ran, grabbed her phone, and dialed both the pastor and Jarrod. When the Pastor and Jarrod arrived, they found Larry passed out in the bathroom. Jarrod quickly dialed 911.

Brandy was frantic, she had no idea what was going on. She followed behind Larry as they placed him in the back of the Ambulance.

"Larry I'm here baby. I'm right here."
The paramedic helped her inside the Ambulance.

Denise Hill- The Seed

Chapter Eleven

At the hospital, Jarrod and the pastor were standing talking as Brandy paced back and forth.

"He wouldn't be in this situation right now if she had been there for him."

Jarrod said loud enough for Brandy to hear.

"How dare you blame this on me!"

"It was your cheating that caused all of this."

"You have no idea what you're talking about. And for your information, I never cheated on Larry."

"Jarrod, you know better than this. This is not the time nor the place for this. You need to apologize to Brandy."

Jarrod hated to admit that he might be wrong, so he walked over to comfort Brandy.

"Brandy, I'm sorry. I had no right accusing you of cheating and blaming you for Larry's illness. I'm just frustrated about all of this and I took it out on you."

Brandy broke down and cried on Jarrod's chest.

"What is going on, Jarrod? Please tell me."

"I think Larry should tell you when he's feeling better."

"No Jarrod, I need to know now."

Just then the doctor came out to the waiting area.

"I take it your Mrs. Jones?"

Brandy shook her head. "How is he?"

"It's touch and go. We've sedated him so he's resting, but his organs are not functioning the way they should, so that's our first concern. We are running several tests to determine the cause of the malfunction. Mrs. Jones, we will do everything we can."

"Can I see him?" Brandy asked.

"Yes, you guys can go back, but like I said, he sedated."

The doctor touched Brandy on the shoulder and walked away.

The three walked into the room. Brandy's heart stopped as she saw Larry laying in the bed.

"Oh my God, Larry. What is going on, baby?"
Brandy moved closer to him. She bent over and kissed Larry on the lips. She stood there looking at her husband. A pang of guilt came over her.

"Maybe Jarrod was right, I should have been there for you instead of worrying about starting my business."

Two hours later, the three stood outside the room.

"Can one of you take me home so I can get my car? I'm going to spend the night with Larry."
They walked down the hall to the elevator, but something caught Jarrod's attention. A woman in a black trench coat with a hood over her head walked by. Something about this woman seemed familiar to him. He turned and watched as she entered the women's bathroom. Something about her nagged at him.

"Pastor, can you take Brandy to get her car while I stay here with Larry until she gets back?"
The pastor looked at Jarrod. He knew he was up to something.

"What is it, Jarrod?"

"Nothing. I will hang around until Brandy gets back."

"Now you know I know you too well. I know when you are lying."

"Pastor, just trust me. Okay."

"Be careful, Jarrod."

"I will. I got this." Jarrod watched as the two entered the elevator. Jarrod walked slowly down the hall and cracked opened Larry's door and stuck his head inside. He saw nothing unusual, so he made his way to stand in front of the women's bathroom where he saw the woman enter.
Jarrod stood there for about a minute before knocking on the door. He knocked twice before pushing the door open.

"Is anyone in here?"

Jarrod asked twice before moving further inside. He continued inside until he could see the sinks. He moved in front of the first stall. He opened the stall slightly with his foot and continued until he reached the last stall. Before Jarrod opened the stall, the door opened swiftly and there stood the woman in the black trench coat.

"You just couldn't leave well enough alone. Could you, Jarrod? Now you're going to get what you asked for."
Before Jarrod can do anything, Alex zoomed in on Jarrod and thrust her fist into his chest and stood there as he flew up against the mirrors, shattering them and falling to the ground. Alex's fingers became like sharp knives. She took one finger and slit Jarrod's throat. She stood above him as he gasped for air and bled to death.
Alex moved his limp body into the stall, locked the door, and crawled over to the other stall. She rinsed herself off and walked out of the bathroom as if nothing had happened.
Alex walked seductively down the hall until she came to Larry's room. Alex cracked the door open and looked around to see if anyone was in sight before entering. Alex closed the door behind her, locked it, and undressed down to her stilettos. She walked over to Larry's bed, removed the covers, hopped onto the bed, and aroused Larry by massaging his penis until it became long and hard and when she was ready, she hopped on top of him and rode him.
Larry's body was aroused to the fullest. It didn't take much to make him come, and when he came, his body went into a convulsion.
Alex quickly hoped off, grabbed her coat, and cracked the door to find the police, nurses, and doctors just down the hall outside of the bathroom. She also heard over the intercom "CODE BLUE".
Alex eased the door shut, put her coat on and hood over her

head, and eased out the door down the hall to the stairs. Alex just missed some nurses and doctor that ran to Larry's room.

Denise Hill- The Seed

Chapter Twelve

Brandy stepped off the elevator to see all the commotion going on.

"Ma'am, can I see some id, and what's your business here?"

"I'm here to see my husband in room 205. What's going on here. Is my husband okay?"
Brandy panicked after seeing the coroner, the police, and all the people in the hall right outside Larry's room.

"James, let her through."
Brandy rushed down the hall and stood outside Larry's room. She was a little hesitant to open the door, fearing the worst. Brandy pushed the door open slowly and was shocked when she saw the doctor and four nurses working with Larry.

"Oh my God!" Brandy yelled as she rushed inside.

"Mrs. Jones, I need for you to wait outside."

"No, I need to be here for my husband. No, please don't make me leave," Brandy cried.

"We will take good care of him, I promise," One of the nurse escorted Brandy outside the room.

"What's going on with my husband?"

"He went into cardiac arrest while you were gone, but we got to him in time. He is resting now."

"Cardiac arrest!"

"Yes, but like I said, he is resting."

"Oh my God! What could have caused him to go into cardiac arrest?"

"We don't know. The doctors are doing some more testing as we speak."

"Jesus Christ! What's going to happen next. What happened to Jarrod, the guy that was here with him?"

"I have no idea. I haven't seen him."

"What's going on here?" Brandy pointed to the body bag on the stretcher.

"I shouldn't be telling you this, but they found someone murdered in the women's restroom, but you didn't hear that from me."

Brandy's mind jumped to Jarrod.

"Jarrod, where are you?" Brandy reached for her purse and dialed his number and on the second ring, James and Brandy heard the ringing of the phone coming through the body bag.

"No Jarrod, No!" Brandy screamed.

Brandy slid to the floor. James rushed over to her and helped her up. Brandy broke loose from him and ran over to the body bag. She unzipped it and screamed when she saw it was Jarrod.

Brandy was talking to the two officers when the pastor and Jarrod's family arrived, along with three other people who she didn't recognize.

Brandy walked over to the pastor and the family.

"I'm so sorry. I don't know what happened or why it happened."

"Jarrod knew what he was getting himself into. I tried to warn him before I left."

"Warn him about what?"

"Brandy, I can't go into that with you right now. I will talk with you about it a little later, but the pastors and I want to pray over Larry, if you don't mind?"

Brandy nodded her head and made her way over to the nurse's station.

"Excuse me, these pastors would like to pray over my husband, will that be okay?"

"Yes, that will be just fine." The nurse smiled at Brandy.

One week later

Larry and Brandy arrived home after Jarrod's funeral. Larry was not 100% better, but he was well enough for the doctor to release him.

They had just left the gravesite where Larry said goodbye to his best friend of twenty years.

Larry and Brandy slowly walked up the walkway and just as Larry stepped foot inside, his phone rang. Larry looked at the number and knew it was Alex, so he deleted the call.

"Who was that?"

"I didn't recognize the number, so I deleted the call."

As Larry and Brandy moved further inside the home, Brandy stopped, looked at Larry, and then asked.

"So are you going to tell me what the hell is going on?"

Larry looked at Brandy,"I guess now is as good as any time."

Larry took a hold of Brandy's hand and guided her to the den. He waited as she took a seat next to him on the couch.

"I guess I need to start from the very beginning."

"Yes, that would be nice."

After explaining things to Brandy, she sat quietly for some time. He knew she needed time to soak everything in.

After Brandy thought things over, she looked at Larry.

"How can we get rid of her?"

"I don't know. Jarrod had reached out to some of his partners that worked on a project like this in college, but now that he's gone I don't know what to do. Now I can only hope that the pastor's colleagues can help."

"Um… let me check the internet to see what I can find to help get rid of this bitch."

Brandy walked over to the desk and turned on the laptop and started typing.

"Alien/Demon, I can't believe this shit is happening. Now I know why she hounded me so much to partner up with her and why she wanted me to spend so much time with Benjamin. She wanted me out of the way so she could do what she wanted to do with you. She kept telling me I needed to learn as much as I could from Benjamin. And in return, you thought I was cheating, and she was trying to have her way with you. Okay, I found something. It says to get rid of an Alien, one has to keep their mind clear of any negativity and to call on the Archangel Michael to protect them and to banish any evil spirit from them."

"Well, the pastor told me that because we were having problems, this was a way for her to enter my dreams at night and have sex with me and because I was being deprived of sex from my wife."
Brandy looked up from the desk to Larry, who was standing right beside her."

"Baby, I am so sorry. I never knew that my actions would have caused all of this. I was only trying to start my business without any help from you. I wanted to show you I could do it. I wanted you to be proud of me, but I acted selfishly and didn't think about your feelings or needs. Larry, please forgive me, I promise I will never allow this to happen again," Brandy said as the tears rolled down her face.
Larry stood there for a minute thinking about whether he should tell her he had sex with Alex.

"What's wrong, Larry?"

"Can I ask you something and be honest? Did you have sex with Benjamin?"

"No, it was strictly business with us. Oh, now I remember what I wanted to ask you before we had to rush you to the hospital. What did Alex mean when she said make sure you tell me about Friday night?"

"Damn," Larry said to himself. He was thinking should I lie or should I come clean.

"I went to dinner with her on Friday night. She wanted to repay me for fixing her flat."

"Is that all?"

"Yes. I promise."

"Babe, can you do me a favor?"

"Sure, what is it?"

"Can you come upstairs and lay with me while I take a quick nap?"

"Yes, baby, I can do that. Is that all you want?"
Brandy stood and moved closer to Larry.

"Yes, for right now." Larry ran his fingers across her lips before bending down to kiss her. Brandy opened her mouth to allow him to enter. The two stood there for minutes just loving each other with their tongue, until Larry felt someone or something staring at him. Larry broke the kiss and looked up and saw Alex standing outside the window.

"What the fuck!"
Larry rushed over to the window.

"What's wrong?"

"I thought I saw Alex standing outside this window."

"Are you serious?"

"Yes. Unless my eyes are playing tricks on me."
When Larry turned to look back at Brandy. Alex popped up and Brandy saw her this time.

"Oh, you stupid bitch!"
Brandy ran to the front door and was going after Alex, but Larry stopped her.

"Don't you understand who and what you're dealing with? You're dealing with an alien or a demon."

"Can't we call the cops?"

"And tell them what, that we have an alien or demon having sex with your husband. I bet that will go over well."

"Well, what are we going to do?"

"We're going to pray and hopefully Pastor Simmons can tell us what to do to get rid of her."
Larry and Brandy made sure they locked the doors and windows before heading upstairs. Larry stripped down to his boxer's and his T-shirt while Brandy settled for one of

his T-shirts. Brandy turned the television on while Larry got some rest.

Denise Hill- The Seed

Chapter Thirteen

Hours later, Larry awakened to the moon shining in the room. He looked around, trying to focus his eye. He was not sure where he was until he noticed Brandy laying next to him asleep. Larry eased out of the bed slowly, trying not to wake Brandy.

Pastor Simmons awakened from a nightmare about Larry and Alex. He turned to look at his wife, who was looking at him because he was screaming in his sleep.

"Honey, what in the world is wrong with you?"

"I had a horrible dream."

"About what?"

The pastor told his wife about Larry and Alex.

"Oh, my God! That sounds like something from a movie."

"I know. I wish it was just a movie."

The pastor got out of bed, walked over to the dresser, and grabbed his cell phone.

"Who are you calling?"

"I have to call and warn Larry. I think he and Brandy are in danger," The pastor replied.

The pastor called Larry, and it went straight to voice mail. He tried calling again and again, but it continued to go to voicemail. He sent Larry a text message. He waited for a few minutes for a response, but when he didn't get one, he decided to pay them a visit.

"Honey, where are you going at this time of night."

"I have to try to help them," The pastor said.

"Can't you call the police?"

"And tell them what? If I haven't called you in 20 minutes, I want you to call the police and tell them what's going on. Here is Larry's address."

The pastor handed her the piece of paper with the address and kissed her goodbye. The pastor grabbed his bible and headed for the door.

"Please be careful," His wife cried out.

Alex stood outside Larry's home and watched as Larry looked out the window. Larry had a bad feeling about something. He could feel that Alex was somewhere close.

As Larry continued to look out the window, Alex made her way across the street and was walking up the walkway. She walked right through the front door and was headed up the stairs. By this time, Alex was in full Alien form with horns, a long tail, and fingers of metal knives. She slowly walked up the stairs taking one step at a time and when she reached the top, she turned back and looked with a smirk on her face.

Larry turned to look at the entryway of the bedroom and just as he turned, he saw a shadow standing in the entryway.

"Who's there?"

"Who else would it be?"

"What do you want, Alex?"

"I want you. I need to carry your seed."

"Why me?"

"You don't know how you got here, do you? Your mom was raped repeatedly like you by my brother and when she gave birth to you, I knew I would someday have your child to live here on earth as you do."

"That's some bullshit and you know it!" Larry yelled. Alex laughed.

"It's true. You have powers that we have, but they haven't taught you how to use them. Your power is in your eyes and your mind."

Every so often one of us comes down and find people to mate with. Soon earth will be filled with our kind."

"And what kind is that?"

"Some call us Demons, some call us Aliens, but we are all the same."

"Well, I am sorry Alex to disappoint you, but you will never carry my seed."

"I hate to burst your bubble, but your seed is already inside me. I just need to fuck you one more time to start her development."

"That will not happen."

"Are you sure about that?"

"Yes, now that I know who you are and what you are. I would never allow you to have my child."

"Silly boy. You cannot stop me. I can do anything I want to you. I've been fucking you in your dreams for weeks and there was nothing you could do about it," Alex said. "You had no clue what was going on, and if I hadn't presented myself to you, you would still be in the dark."

"Well, it stops tonight. I am asking you to leave my home and never return."

"I'm sorry, but I can't do that. I need you one more time."

Alex zoomed in on Larry. She was now standing directly in front of him and puts him in a trance as she laid him down and undressed him. She climbed on top of him and inserted him inside of her. Alex screamed.

"Oh my God! Yes, you feel so good." Alex was almost there when Brandy awoke. Brandy looked around the room for Larry when she saw this ugly-looking creature.

"Oh my God!"

Alex looked up at Brandy and smiled.

"Yes!!!"

Brandy ran over to Alex and Larry, Alex pushed her hand out and threw Brandy up against the wall. And after Alex was finished with Larry, she got up and moved toward Brandy, who was still laying on the ground.

"Larry, Larry, Larry, wake up!" Brandy yelled.

Larry stirred awake and saw Alex heading toward Brandy.
He slowly got up off the ground and pull his boxers up
and tried to stop Alex, but Larry was no match for her. She
reached down for Brandy and picked her up and threw her
across the room. Alex then stuck her claws into her thigh
and continued to claw her.

"Ah! Stop you psychotic bitch!"
Larry yelled. "Leave her alone!"
The sound of Larry's voice irritated Alex. She stopped
stabbing Brandy and approached Larry.

"Stay the hell away from him." Brandy yelled.
The pastor pulled into Larry's driveway, cut the engine,
and hopped out. He ran to the front door and turned the
knob, but it was locked. He pulled out his phone and called
Larry, again and again, and each time it went to voicemail.
The pastor pounded on the front door, hoping Brandy or
Larry will hear him, but unfortunately his knocks went
unheard. The pastor went around to the side window, broke
the glass with his bible, and went inside.

Alex looked back at Brandy and went over to her and
grabbed Brandy by the throat and lifted her off the floor.
She allowed Brandy's body to dangle for a minute before
throwing her across the room, and against the dresser
hitting her head against the mirror shattering it to pieces
and watching her limp body hit the floor.

"Get the fuck out of here, you got what you wanted."
Alex moved closer to Larry just as the pastor appeared in
the door's entryway.

"Alex, stop! I rebuke you in the name of Jesus Christ."
The pastor held a gold cross in his hand. Alex looked at the
pastor sideways and slowly moved toward him.

"Stop, I demand you!"
Alex stood directly in front of the pastor, looking at him as
if he had three heads. Then, out of nowhere, she stuck her
claws into his stomach. When she pulled her claws out, she

pulled out some of his intestines and licked them off her claws.

Larry looked at her in disbelief. He couldn't believe what he was seeing.

The pastor fell to the ground, Alex turned back to look at Larry as she showed him her pregnant stomach.

Alex rubbed her stomach and laughed as she exited the room. Larry laid his head back against the wall, trying to convince himself that this was just a bad dream, but when Brandy came and called out to him, he knew this was all too real.

"Baby, what just happened?" Brandy asked as she crawled over to him. Brandy looked up at him. Brandy saw Larry had been wounded in the shoulder and thigh.

"Are you okay?"

Larry nodded his head yes. Brandy looked over at the pastor and saw him lying in a puddle of blood, she screamed.

"Oh my God! Oh my God!"

Brandy continued to scream.

"Brandy, baby, calm down."

Denise Hill- The Seed

Chapter Fourteen

The paramedics and the police arrived along with the pastor's wife. She called them as directed by her husband since she had not heard from him. The police officers entered the house with their guns drawn as they heard Brandy's screams coming from upstairs. The officers enter the bedroom to find the pastor dead and Brandy and Larry laying up against the wall.

"Are you guys okay?"

"My wife needs medical attention."

"What about you?" The second officer said.

Larry pointed to his chest.

Mrs. Simmons made her way upstairs and saw her husband's body.

"Oh my God! No, no honey, no!"

"Ma'am, you shouldn't be in here," The first officer said.

They put Brandy and Larry in the same hospital room. They were told by the doctor that the police wanted to speak to them.

"The police are outside in the hall waiting to speak with you two, so just let me know when you're ready. In the meantime, I think there's someone who I know you will want to speak to also outside in the hall. I will bring her in."

The doctor escorted Mrs. Simmons in. As she walked over to the two, you can see the sadness in her eyes.

"Good afternoon," You two.

"Good afternoon, Mrs. Simmons. You know, we both are so sorry about what happened to the pastor. I feel responsible for his death. If I hadn't brought this to him, he would still be here."

The tears rolled down Brandy's face.

"I'm so sorry for your loss, Mrs. Simmons. Your husband was such a good man, and I know he will be missed by many. If there's ever anything that my husband and I can do, just let us know," Brandy said.

"I appreciate that, but my husband knew what he was getting himself into. But there's one thing you guys can do for me and yourself," Mrs. Simmons said.

"What is that, Mrs. Simmons?" Larry asked.

"Let's get our story together because you have the police and reporters right outside this room. Now I told the police that my husband rushed to your home because he felt you guys were in trouble and when he got there, he could tell that an intruder was inside with you guys and that's when I called the police. Whatever you do, you can't tell them the truth because you guys know how this will look to everyone," Mrs. Simmons said.

"Right!" Larry responded.

"So you guys need to come up with a description of the person and a reason you think he was there, or that it was just a burglary and that my husband walked in on it and was stabbed to death," Mrs. Simmons told them.

"Okay, do you need help with the funeral arrangements?" Brandy asked.

"No, my kids are on their way here to help me out. My daughter wants me to move in with her and my grandkids. I will put the house on the market sometime next month. I will call you guys a little later this evening."

Mrs. Simmons walks over to Larry and kissed him on his cheek. She looked over at Brandy, who had tears in her eyes and moved over to her and kissed her on the cheek.

"Oh, sweetheart, don't cry. Everything happens for a reason. My husband is in a better place now. I don't know if you guys knew this or not, but he had stage four cancer and was given approximately 6 months to live. My husband lived his life to the fullest, and he died doing what he did best, and that was helping people."

"Man, we never knew that," Larry said.

"He hid a lot of things from people. He wanted no one to feel sorry for him. My husband was a strong man until the end.

"Yes, he was," Brandy said.

Just then two police officers walked in. Mrs. Simmons winked at the couple and walked out.

The two police officers walked over and stood in the middle of both beds.

"How are you guys doing?" The first Officer asked.

"We've been better," Larry said.

"We are sorry about your pastor and I know this may not be a good time, but we need to get your story on what happened. We talked with Mrs. Simmons last night and she filled us in on what she could," The second Officer said.

"So, the intruder. Did you recognize him and can you give us a description of him?"

Denise Hill- The Seed

Chapter Fifteen

Two weeks later, Larry made the dreadful call to his mom, who lived an hour away.

"Mom, I need some answers. I need to know about my dad. I've been going through some things and I met someone that told me things that I need clarification on."

Larry's mom Lisa dreaded this phone call. She knew someday she would get this call.

"Do you and Brandy have time to come down for a visit? I would rather tell you this in person."

The next day, Larry and Brandy arrive at his mom's. He was a little on edge. He was not sure if he really wanted to know the truth, but he was there now.

"Oh, my God! I am so glad to see the two of you."

"Hey, Mrs. Jones, how have you been?"

"I'm doing good for an old lady."

"Hey, Mom."

"Hey mom nothing, you better get your butt over here and hug me. And why don't I have any grandchildren yet?"

Larry looked over at Brandy.

"Don't you dare look at me!"

The three laughed.

"Well, come on and have a seat I know you want to know some things, but let me bring out the lunch that I made for us."

Larry's mom explained.

"Let's see, where should I begin. Thirty-five years ago, I gave birth to you. Your birth wasn't normal by any means. I had you two weeks after I found out I was pregnant, but by this time, my husband had left me for another woman so I didn't have to explain anything to him, but before that all happened, I started having terrible nightmares, or at least that's what I thought they were. I would always dream that someone was having sex with me while I was sleep, and I

86

just thought it was your dad. You know he worked nights so a lot of times he would come home and while I was sleep he would take care of his needs. So one particular morning, I awoke, and I was so sore I could barely move. I immediately asked your dad to not be so rough. He had no idea what I was talking about, he said he hadn't touched me in a couple of weeks, which was odd because he had a high sex drive, but anyway, at first, I thought he was lying, but one night when he went back home to visit his mom in the hospital, it happened again and I knew it wasn't him because this person was much larger. When your dad got back, I tried to tell him what was happening, but he didn't believe me. In the meantime, he started hanging out more after work and eventually I caught him cheating on me with some young girl named Alex. She helped tear our marriage apart. That's when I met this man. I thought he was my knight in shining armor, boy was I wrong, he turned out to be the person who was raping me in my dreams. He later revealed himself to me, and what I saw scared the living daylights out of me. He was an alien. He had impregnated me with you. He told me many half aliens and half-human people were walking around on earth and someday soon they would take over the earth. When you were born, they drew some blood from your arm and that triggered a red flag. For the first five years of your life, we were on the run from the government. Whenever this happens, they will send these government officials out to take the baby from the mother and hide the baby from the world so that no one knows what's going on and they experiment on them."

Larry stood and walked over to look out the window. He couldn't believe what he had just heard, but as he continued to look, he noticed a black unmarked government official car parked two houses down.

Larry turned to look back at his mom.

"Mom, has anyone visited you lately? I mean, have you seen anything out of the ordinary?" Larry asked.

"No, why you ask?"

"There's a black unmarked car parked two houses down. It looks like a government official car."

"Come to think of it, I noticed that car. It has been here for a week now, but I have not seen anyone one get in or get out.

Larry turned his attention back to the car and saw two white men get out with weapons. He watched them closely until they came and stood at his mom's house.

"Shit! We have got to get out of here!" Larry yelled.

"What's going on?" His mom asked.

"Someone knows we are here!"

"Here, you guys take my car." Larry's mom said as she reached into her purse and handed him the keys.

"No, mom you're coming with us."

"Don't worry about me, I will be fine. Now go!"

"I'm not leaving without you!"

"I'm much too old to be on the run anymore."

"Mom, I'm not leaving without you, so let's go!"

Brandy grabbed Mrs. Jones by the arm as they moved toward the back door. They run out to the detached car garage in the back where Mrs. Jones parked her car. Larry hopped in on the driver's side as he told the two women to get in the back.

"I need for you guys to duck down until we get to our car and once we get there, Mom, I want you and Brandy to ride together in my car. Mom, I am so glad you had me park the car around the corner," Larry said as he looked back at his mom.

"How did you know they would show up?"

"When you called and told me you had been sick and that you had been to the doctor, I knew once they had drawn your blood that it would raise a red flag. This is the same thing that happened to me when you were born. They came after me. They wanted you. The government wanted to take you away and keep you hidden away from the world so they could treat you like a guinea pig. My mom made us leave the state. She sent me to a place in North Dakota that helped people in my situation, but after being there for a year, the government found out about the place and killed the people in charge and most of the people that were hiding out there. So we were on the run again. We were on the run for another four years until I came to Atlanta, Indiana. It was much smaller than it is today. I had no issues with anyone. I got a job quickly, and I settled down here. Back then it was only 4 black people here when we came."

"Are you serious?"

"It's only about 10 black people now."

"Tell her, Larry. Larry didn't leave here until he went to college. I thought we were safe, but I guess I was wrong."

"I always wondered why my granny, aunts, and uncle's never came to visit and why I could only talk to them over the phone. Come to think of it, we never used our home phone we always used a payphone far from our home."

"It wasn't safe. I didn't want the government a to find us. I made that mistake once when we were in Dakota. Believe it or not, Benjamin helped us out in many situations that could have turned deadly, including the Dakota situation."

"Who is this Benjamin?" Larry asked.

His mom hesitated in answering, "He's your dad... the alien."

Larry stopped the car in the middle of the street.

"So, it's true what Alex told me?"

"Alex, who is Alex?" His mom asked.

"She's the lady that has been having sex with me in my dream."

"Oh my God! Did you get her pregnant?" His mom asked.

Denise Hill- The Seed

Chapter Sixteen

The two white government officials kicked in the door and searched each room before heading out to the backyard

"Dammit! I know they were here."

"How can you be so sure? We did not see them enter," The second official asked.

"I just know this is where they were."

"Well, it looks like you were wrong. Let's stop wasting our time here," The second official said.

The first officer was pissed and started walking away. The second officer followed behind him with a smirk on his face as a glimpse of his body transformed into an alien and then back to a human.

Brandy and her mother-in-law got into Larry's car and follow behind Larry until they reached their home in Indianapolis.

Larry pulled into the alley and parked his car in the backyard. Brandy pulled alongside of him.

"You guys stay here until I know it's safe to go inside."

Larry eased the back door open and made his way inside the house. He looked around and listened for any sound of movement. He noticed the front door was slightly cracked open. He stood there, unsure of what to do when he sees a shadow moving down the stairs and toward him, and as it got closer and closer, the shadow transformed into Benjamin.

"What the hell! Benjamin, what are you doing here?"

"I mean you no harm son, I only here to help."

"I'm not your son!"

Benjamin laughed.

"Why don't you tell your mother and wife to come inside."

"How did you know my mom is outside?"

"Son, I know more than you think."

The ladies walked inside, and immediately Brandy saw Benjamin.

"Ben, what are you doing here?" Brandy asked.

Mattie looked at Brandy, "You two know each other? Ben, tell me you didn't?"

"Hello Mattie, good to see you too and yes, we know each other, and no I didn't."

"I'm so confused. What the hell is going on?" Larry said.

"Remember when I mentioned Benjamin, Larry, this is your father."

"Are you serious?" It shocked Larry.

Heads turn when Alex walked down the stairs with an infant.

"Hello Larry, say hello to your daughter, Geneva," Alex said, smiling

"Okay, it's time to get serious guys," Larry said as he laughed.

Benjamin heard a car pull up outside and walked over to the window and looked out.

"There's no time to explain we have company. Alex, I need you out back with the cars and I need all of you to sit on the couch and keep quiet."

Alex handed Larry baby Geneva as she walked out back. Benjamin created an invisible shield around them. The two government officials kicked open the door with their weapons drawn.

"I'll check upstairs while you check downstairs," One officials said. The other official looked over at the invisible shield and winked.

"Everything's clear down here," One man yelled.

"It's all clear upstairs. Where in the hell can they be?" He asked as he walked back downstairs.

"I told you I saw them heading north, but you still insist on coming here."

The officials walked outside and stood on the porch for a few minutes before heading back to the office.

Minutes later, when the coast was clear, Alex walked back inside and Benjamin broke the invisible shield.

"Tell me what just happened here?" Larry asked.

"It's a long story," Benjamin said as he looked over at Mattie. "You guys need to get out of here. Pack as much as you can. I have a place where you can stay and where you will be safe."

"Hell Naw! I'm not going anywhere with her," he pointed at Alex. "She killed my best friend and my pastor," Larry yelled.

"I'm sorry Larry, but you have to understand, I wasn't myself, once the transformation takes place, there's only one thing on our mind and whoever gets in your way, well, you know the rest."

"Once you learn your powers, Larry, you will understand," Benjamin said.

Alex walked over and picked up Geneva, "She looks so much like you."

"Can I hold her?" Mattie asked.

"Sure, you can hold your grandbaby."

Larry wasn't ready to claim the child just yet. He looked over at his mom and shook his head.

"Larry, I know it's hard for you to believe, trust me, I know. I struggled to believe it when I had you. I prayed that this would never happen to you. I guess I should have told you about this beforehand."

Larry sat there in silence, looking at the baby, and then he looked over at his wife, Brandy.

She laid her hand on top of his, "It's hard for you to believe, but just think about how this feels to me," She shook her head. "I guess it will be an adjustment for all of us."

Denise Hill- The Seed

Chapter Seventeen

Once everyone had packed Larry and Brandy followed behind Benjamin and Alex while Mattie followed behind them. They drove for about an hour and a half to a rural area on the outskirts of Indiana. Once they came to a wooded bridge, they took a left turn onto a dirt-covered road that led into the woods. They drove another twenty minutes until they came to a big wired fence. They went inside, where they saw a compound that looked like a big warehouse or some school. It stunned the three because on the outside the compound was invisible to the eye until you were behind the fence.

Alex took baby Geneva inside for her feeding, while Benjamin showed the three around and explained everything to them.

"Tomorrow," Benjamin said as he looked at Larry, "I will show you where you will begin your training."

"Training, what training?"

Benjamin laughed.

"You do not understand what powers you possess, do you?"

Larry looked at Benjamin. He didn't know if he should like him or not.

"You guys are free to come and go as you please, but you will have to make sure no one follows you back here. We have a curfew and if you're not back in time, you will have to find your way in because the gate will be invisible."

"And what time is that?" Larry asked.

"10 pm. Alex and I will go back home within the next week and we will not be back until mating season or if someone needs our help. Also, dinner will be ready in about an hour, so I will take you to your rooms and let you get situated.

Before arriving at their rooms, Benjamin showed them an area that looked like a cafeteria.

"Dinner will be served in this area here."

"Thank you, Benjamin," Mattie said as she smiled at him.

Truth be told, Mattie still cared for him even though she knew what he was. There were many times he had come to their rescue when Larry was younger. He had spent countless hours with them, but Mattie failed to realize was Benjamin had fathered many children while on earth, so Larry was not his only child.

Once inside their room, Larry walked over to their window and looked out, "I feel like I'm in a bad dream and I can't wake up."

"Well, babe, I'm sorry to tell you, it's not a dream."

"Did you see how my mom talked to him? She acts like she still has feelings for him even after what he has done to her, I mean us."

"You know, I'm going to laugh to keep from crying right now." Brandy said.

Larry walked over to her, "Come here, sweetheart. I'm so sorry that you have to deal with this. We don't have to stay here if you don't want to. We can always leave town or go back home, and I can take my chances with the government finding me."

"Now you know I wouldn't put your life in jeopardy like that."

"What is the worst thing that the government can do to me, besides kill me?"

"Larry, stop it!"

"I'm just saying."

"I'm going to take a shower before dinner," Brandy said.

"Why don't you get some rest while I'm in the shower."

Larry laid on the bed. He had so many things on his mind that he couldn't sleep even if he wanted to.

Once Brandy finished showering, Larry showered. As Brandy was dressing, she felt eyes on her and when she looked up, there was Benjamin.

"Shh, I will not hurt you." He said as he moved closer to her.

"Stay away from me!" Brandy covered her breasts with her hands.

Benjamin stood there and with his hands slowly touching her nipples. His touch was so gentle and his fingers were so soft. She felt nothing like it. His eyes seemed to put her in a trance because she couldn't move all she could do was to watch as he raped her with his mind. She felt his lips on her mouth, but he hadn't moved. How was that possible she thought? Then he moved to her breasts and licked each nipple. And last she could feel his lips on her nub. The feeling was so amazing.

"Oh my God!" She screamed. And then the orgasm shook her entire body. And just like that, he was gone, and she fell onto the bed.

"Hey, what's wrong?" Larry asked as he walked out of the bathroom.

Brandy lay on the bed motionless, "Hey, are you okay?"

Minutes later she spoke, "We got to get out of here," She said as the tears rolled down her face.

"Did something happen?" Larry reached over and hugged her.

"He, he raped me without touching me!"

"Who did?"

"Your father, Benjamin."

Larry slowly released her. He couldn't believe what was happening.

"I'll kill him!"

"No, you're no match for him."

"I have to learn how to use my powers and then I will kill that bitch!"

Larry looked over at Brandy, "I'm sorry baby, I am sorry I got you mixed up in this bullshit." Larry pulled her into his arms.

"I want to go home."

"I know, so do I. I want my life back no matter how fucked up it was."

"I say we leave now and just take our chances," Brandy said.

"I agree. Let's find mom first."
Brandy got dressed, and they left out to find his mom so they could leave.
They searched her room, but she was not there, so they headed for the dining area. They found her sitting with Benjamin.

"Mom, let's go."

"Where are we going?"

"We are going back home. We will take our chances and if the government finds us, so be it."

"Nonsense. They will find you in no time, and besides, I have to finish mating with your wife." Benjamin said.
Larry lunged for Benjamin, but he jumped back.

"You son of a bitch! You leave my wife alone. Haven't you and your sister done enough already?"
Everyone turned to look.

"Larry, my boy. Don't take it personally, this is what we do while on earth."

"I'm warning you, leave her alone!"
Benjamin reached inside his pocket and pulled out the keys to Larry's car.

"Once you leave, you are on your own. And what about Geneva?"

"She's not mine and she's not my problem."

"What if your mom would have felt the same way about you?"

"I wish she would have."

"Now baby, you don't mean that." His mom said."

"Son, just know you are always welcome here. And remember, at 10 pm the force field is around the building so you won't be able to see the entrance so before you go, make yourself familiar with the opening, just in case you need to come back after 10."

"I'm going to stay."

"Mom!"

"Honey, I'm too old for all of this. I feel safe here."

"You can always come and visit her," Benjamin said as he looked directly at Brandy. Brandy moved to stand behind Larry.

They said their goodbyes and were on their way.

Denise Hill- The Seed

Chapter Eighteen

Two weeks later, Brandy nightmares had begun. She had dreams of Benjamin having sex with her and when she awakened; she was moist and sore, so she knew she was not dreaming.

"Babe, you don't look so hot. Are you feeling okay?" Larry asked Brandy.

"No, I feel horrible. I'm afraid what Alex did to you, Benjamin, is doing to me in my sleep."

"What! I told that mutherfucker to leave you alone. I see I am going to have to visit."

"Is it really going to help, no!"

"There has got to be something we can do."

"Prayer. I was looking on the internet again and found that if you put salt around your home and burn sage, it would keep evil spirits away."

"But will it keep aliens away?"

Brandy replied, "I don't know, but it won't hurt to try."

Over the weeks, Brandy's nightmares had gotten worse and one night she swore she saw Benjamin in their bedroom.

She had just awakened from one of her many nightmares about him, but this dream was different, it felt so real, she could feel him penetrate her and the size was way too big, but the feeling was out of this world and when he finished she woke and thought she saw him standing at their bedroom door. The more she looked at him, the more he disappeared.

That night she told Larry about what she thought happened.

"Are you serious?"

"Yeah, and I didn't want to tell you. Do you think he impregnated me?"

"Yes, that's exactly what happened with me and Alex."

I can't believe him. I should go to the police and have his ass arrested."

They both looked at each other and laughed.

"I know this is not a laughing matter, but just hearing myself say that is kind of stupid."

"Yeah, what are you going to tell them, that an alien raped my wife?"

"Come here, I'm so sorry you have to go through this. If I had known about this in the beginning, I wouldn't have married you, hell I wouldn't have married anyone."

Larry hugged his wife as she lay her head on his chest.

The next day, Brandy went into work and everyone was talking about how the new boss just up and disappeared.

"Well, if you ask me, I'm glad his ass is gone."

"I thought you two got along very well. If we didn't know any better, we would have thought you guys were dating." Shanice said.

"Yeah, right."

"Brandy, are you feeling well?" Gloria asked.

"No, I'm not feeling well at all."

"What's wrong?" Shanice asked.

"If you only knew."

"Come on, tell us what's going on. Are you pregnant? We used to tell each other everything," Gloria said.

Just then a black female appeared.

"Hey ladies, my name is Lisa Vincent. I will fill in while Benjamin is away."

Lisa eyed Brandy suspiciously.

"Damn, girl, do you know her?"

"No, but she looks familiar."

"She eyed you like you stole her man or something."

"I know, what's up with that?" Brandy asked.

Later that day, Lisa called Brandy into her office.

"Have a seat," Lisa said as she pointed to the chair in front of the desk.

"Benjamin told me all about you, Brandy. And just remember that it would not benefit you or anyone here if anyone found out about us. Now, are we on the same page?"

Brandy shook her head yes.

"Well, now that we both understand, we are done here, but I will keep a close eye on you."

When Brandy walked back to her desk, her Co-workers were all eyes and ears.

"So, what was that all about," Shanice asked as she stood up from her cubical and looked over at Brandy?"

"She just wanted to let me know that Benjamin had nothing but good things to say about me and that if she needed anything she was to come to me."

Brandy sat for the next hour wondering if she could go anywhere and not be found by these people.

Larry was on his way home from work when he saw a black Lincoln Town car that looked like a government official car tailing him. He turned left; the car turned left. He turned right; the car turned right. Larry took a quick right and sped up and turn into an alley and waited to see if the car was following him and when the car rode past the alley, he had his answer.

He pulled out his phone and called Brandy.

"Hey, have you left work yet?"

"No, I am walking to my car now."

"Don't go home, meet me at the Court Yard hotel on 86th and Allisonville."

"Why, what's going on?"

"I think some men from the government followed me from work, but I lost them."

"Well, you will not believe who showed up for worked today as Benjamin's temporary replacement."

"Who?"

"One of them. Her name is Lisa Vincent. I will tell you all about it when I see you."

"Okay, just be careful and make sure no one follows you."

"Okay, babe, love you."

When they arrived at The Court Yard, Brandy got out of her car and got into the car with Larry.

"Now, what?"

"Your guess is as good as mine. I want to wait until it's dark to go home. We can sneak in through the back. Are you hungry?"

"No, I couldn't even eat lunch."

"Brandy, you have to eat something or you will starve and end up in the hospital as I did."

"Okay, let's go eat."

Brandy and Larry were sitting in Outback eating when two men dressed in black walked in. Larry remembered them from the house.

"Johnny, why don't you go that way and I will go over here," Frank said.

Frank quickly made his way over to Brandy and Larry.

"You guys need to leave right away and head for the Compound now! I will take care of the bill."

Brandy and Larry rushed out of the restaurant and jumped in their car, but they were so busy trying to escape, they never notice another car with a man inside watching them. When they pulled off, he pulled off.

It took them some time to get to the compound, but when they did, Benjamin and some others were there at the gate waiting for them.

The man following them stopped and cut his car off and watched. He watched as Larry's car drove inside, and all at once, there was nothing there. He blinked his eyes a couple of times.

"What the hell!"
He got out of his car and walked a half a mile to where he saw the car enter. He looked around as he ran his hand through his hair.
He walked back to his car and drove back to where he saw the car enter. He tried to drive his car in but ran into the force field and dented his bumper.
Larry, Brandy, Benjamin, and two others stood and watched the man.

"You two go on in and get some dinner while we handle the situation."
Once Brandy and Larry were safely inside, Benjamin released the force field and allow the man to drive through. Once he was through, Benjamin grabbed the man out of the car and starred him dead in his eyes, and his eyes burned a hole through the man's forehead, just as he did Luke.

The End